For C.H.

Kids Can Press acknowledges the financial support of the Government of Ontario, through the Ontario Media Development Corporation's Ontario Book Initiative; the Ontario Arts Council; the Canada Council for the Arts; and the Government of Canada, through the BPIDP, for our publishing activity.

Published in Canada by
Kids Can Press Ltd.
29 Birch Avenue
Toronto, ON M4V 1E2

Published in the U.S. by
Kids Can Press Ltd.
2250 Military Road
Tonawanda, NY 14150

www.kidscanpress.com

Edited by Karen Li
Designed by Kathleen Gray
Printed and bound in Singapore

The hardcover edition of this book is smyth sewn casebound.
The paperback edition of this book is limp sewn with drawn-on cover.

CM 09 0 9 8 7 6 5 4 3 2 1
CM PA 09 0 9 8 7 6 5 4 3 2 1

Library and Archives Canada Cataloguing in Publication

Poon, Janice
Claire and the water wish / Janice Poon.

Target audience: For ages 7–10.
ISBN 978-1-55453-381-7 (bound). ISBN 978-1-55453-382-4 (pbk.)

1. Pollution—Comic books, strips, etc. I. Title.

PS8631.O638C533 2009 j741.5'971 C2008-903252-7

Kids Can Press is a Corus™ Entertainment company

Claire and the Water Wish

Written and illustrated by

JANICE POON

Kids Can Press

Dear Diary:

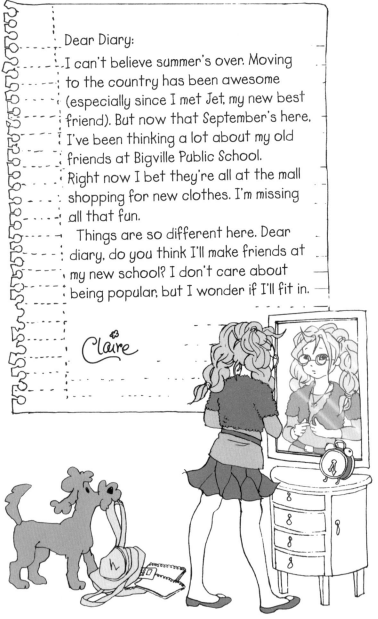

I can't believe summer's over. Moving to the country has been awesome (especially since I met Jet, my new best friend). But now that September's here, I've been thinking a lot about my old friends at Bigville Public School. Right now I bet they're all at the mall shopping for new clothes. I'm missing all that fun.

Things are so different here. Dear diary, do you think I'll make friends at my new school? I don't care about being popular, but I wonder if I'll fit in.

Claire

Wish me luck, Bongo.

Claire!
Thanks for saving me a seat, Jet.
There's something I want to show you.

Do you know all these kids?
Just a sec ...
Hi, Claire. This is Tabby. She lives over by the Perkins'.

Claire's my new neighbor. She was on TV this summer. She rescued her mom from a kidnapper.

I like your backpack. Is that a TinkiToy? You should hang it on your lunch box. See mine?

That's cute. I don't use a lunch box. At Bigville Public, everyone carries lunch in their backpack.

Everyone *here* uses a lunch box.

It's what's inside that worries me. My mom is vegan. I usually trade.

Actually, my mom is a food expert. My lunch is always gourmet.

Want some gum?

Well, maybe the gum's not gourmet. But everything else is.

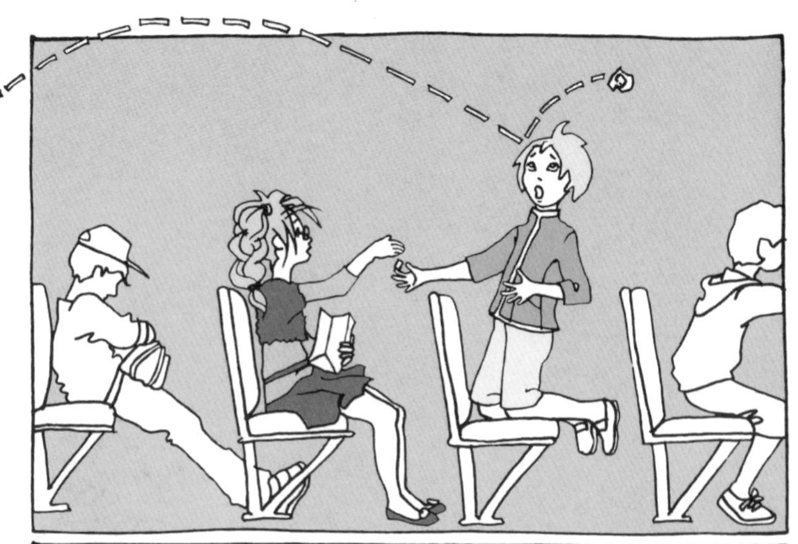

You loser!

Those creeps from smelly Lovesick Lake are totally out of control.

They've probably been on this bus since *dawn*. Lovesick Lake is practically in the Arctic, y'know.

Well they should GROW UP or move closer to school.

Found it! Hey, Claire, look at this!
WIN A KIDCAM
WRITE AN ESSAY ON AN ENDANGERED SPECIES
TOP TEN ESSAYS will WIN a SUPER DIGITAL CAMERA!
ENTER NOW!

Just what I need — a camera. I was thinking that if you were going to be a zoologist like Dr. Jane Goodall, I could be a wildlife photographer like "Nick" Nichols, and we could start a magazine just like *National Geographic*.
But you have to write an essay. You hate writing.
But I love contests.

I just have to think of a really winning topic. Something popular.
How about "Saving the Princess of Whales"?
Be serious! I really need this camera. Help me think of a topic.
Pandas, penguins ...

... snow leopards, gray wolves ...
Not colorful enough.
African lions, Bengal tigers, deep sea squid.
Something closer to home ...

We're in classroom 5B.

What about Monarch butterflies?

Are they going extinct?

By the time you write this essay, they could be.

Dear Diary:

School here is better than I imagined. Everyone's pretty friendly, and I really like Ms. Beene, my teacher. I hope I do okay in her class. I don't want her to think I'm an idiot – which I'm not.

Jet is totally obsessed with the camera contest. That's all she talks about now. There are only ten prizes being awarded in the whole school district, but she's positive she's going to win one. That's Jet, no doubt!

Claire

A Few Weeks Later ...
All right, class. For your next assignment, I want you to split up into groups of three or four.

Partners, okay?
Okay. Partners.
QUIETLY!
How come she always shouts when she says "Quietly"?

Who should we get for the rest of our group?
Hey, Jet!
I think Tabby ...

Now. Who needs another partner?
Excellent. Sky, you can fill in your brother and cousin once they are well enough to come back to school.

Let's see. What topic would make a really great diorama? Sky, can you draw?

If I had my camera we wouldn't have to draw. We could just take photos and they would be perfect.

Do you have a camera?
Not yet. I need an essay topic first. Passenger pigeons are already extinct. Puffins? Ptarmigans?
Why don't we do our project on water? At my old school I did a report called "The Water Cycle," and I got an "A."
I like water. My dad says that the way we live depends on where our water comes from.

Extinct ... colorful ... close to home ...
"Where Our Water Comes From" is a really good topic. What do you think, Jet?
Later. I'm getting a huge brainwave ...
Guess it's up to you and me. Contest Girl is tuned to her inner radio.

Dear Diary:

Big news! Jet won the contest – and the camera! She wrote an essay on how the family farm is like an endangered species. Ms. Beene always says to write about what you know, and it worked! No wonder Jet's been so sneaky lately. She never showed me her essay or anything before she handed it in. She said I've been too busy with Sky. What's that supposed to mean?

Claire

LATER THAT WEEKEND ...
FLASH!
FLASH!
FLASH!

Strike a pose!
Cut it out, Jet. I'm trying to give Bongo his bath.
I'll call this photo "How Wolf Became Man's Best Friend."

Bongo! Oh, no!
Jet. Help me!

These are called "candid shots."

Hold it ... smile ... now look angry.

Give me that thing. See how you like "candid shots."

How does this work?
Here. Just look in the back. See? Then push this button.
What are these buttons for?
They're for zooming in or zooming out. For close-up or faraway things.
Like a bug or a mountain?
Who knows? I take pictures of people. I'm a people person.

Are there instructions?
Here.
Manual

Hmmmm.

Figured it out yet?
Let me see.

Slide this button.

Press that one.

Move your head. I'm going to take a picture of those birds on Mrs. Potts' washline.
That's so cool. Do you want to bike over to our lookout and see what kind of close-up and faraway pictures we can get?
Naw. I've got to get home.

But you can borrow my camera 'til tomorrow.
Are you sure?

Yes. I'm helping Mom box vegetables tonight. She's paying me so I can buy a camera bag.

A camera bag?
It's part of my new look.

Like that old hat you've been wearing every day?
It's not old. It's artistic. And it's French. It's pronounced ber-ay. I saw it in a magazine.
Oh, now you speak French.
If you can say gourmet, I can say beret.
Well, my mom IS a gourmet.
Well I AM an artist.

I have to go.
Maybe you can get some close-ups of the moon tonight.

Can it take pictures that far away?

I dunno, but it's the kind of thing you'd try.

THE NEXT DAY ...
Strike a pose!
Make it happen!
You're it!

Miss Jet, I hope I will be seeing the fruit of all this photography in your project.
BZZZZZ ZZZZZZ
Now, don't forget. You will be presenting your dioramas to the whole class next week.

Our diorama is ready.
It's going to be the most
fabulous.
And the
biggest!
The biggest is not
always the best.
We'll see. 
C'mon, boys!

We'd better get going on our presentation. Let's take our diorama to my place and work on it together over the weekend.

I can get my Dad to drive me in on Saturday.
Okay, Jet?

I can't. I promised Tabby and Erica I'd take some pictures of them.

Well, I guess it's up to us, Sky. Why don't you sleep over? Then we can work on it all weekend.
Oh, I'd love that. I think my dad will let me.
I can try to help Sunday ...

Forget it.
I'm *sure* Tabby and Erica will want tons and tons of pictures.

Dear Diary:

Things have gotten so mixed up ever since Jet won that camera. Now she only wants to hang with the popular kids. I think they're just using her to get pictures of themselves. Maybe tomorrow when we're at the market – where there aren't any cliques – we'll have fun together like we used to.

Claire

GOOD OLD FUN AHEAD TO MARKET

THE NEXT DAY...
PICK 'N' SAVE
MARKET

Before you girls run off, help me unload these vegetables.
Hi, Lucy! Got something for me to sell?
Hi, Fred! I've made up mixed boxes of vegetables, duck eggs and fresh cheese. I hope the weekend will be busy. We could sure use the extra cash.

Oh, it's gonna be real busy. Lotsa city folk tearin' up the road to see the fall colors.
They can come as often as they like as long as they keep buying my market boxes.
Here, Jet. Some vegetable money to add to your Camera Bag Fund.
You, too, Claire — for helping unload the boxes.
Now be back here in half an hour.
Thanks, Mom. C'mon, Claire, let's go!
Thanks, Mrs. Diaz.

That's where they have some really cool stuff.
I hope we can find some cute lunch boxes.
I thought you said lunch boxes were for kindergarten.

FLEA MARKET

WELCOME TO PICK 'N' SAVE

I guess it depends ... if the style is cute, a lunch box is okay.

They're better than those paper bags of yours.

Your sandwiches are always squished. What about a Thermos?

I'll never use a Thermos.

Oh ... My ... Gosh.
Look, Claire. It's fantabulastic.
The blue one?

Oh, I love it.

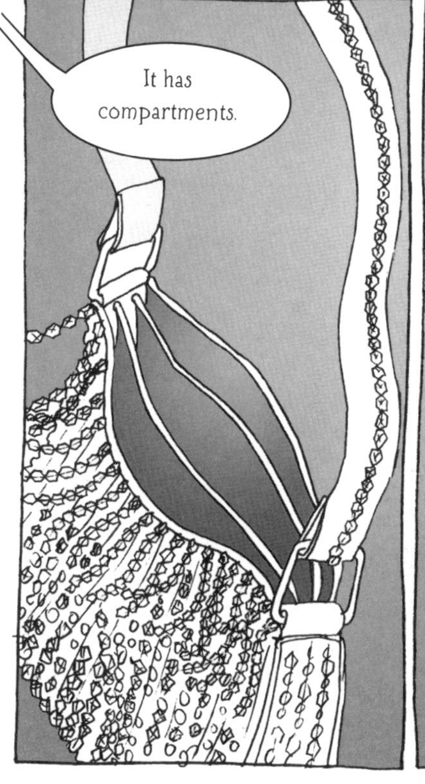
It has compartments.

Excellent for my attachments if I get any.

It's not a camera bag, it's a purse.
It's so sparkly and totally covered in jewels. It's bedazzled!
They're not jewels. They're plastic ...
Look at the price. That's exactly how much I have. I'm getting it.
Why don't you get one in denim?

Denim is dull. This bag has "flair."

Yeah, like an emergency flare. We'll never lose you in the snow with that thing around your neck.

You're serious ...

Claire, this is the new me. You're too busy hanging out with Sky to notice.

I've become more sophisticated since photography has opened my eyes. People change.
Look at you. You're carrying a lunch box now And I'm the one who look like a city girl.

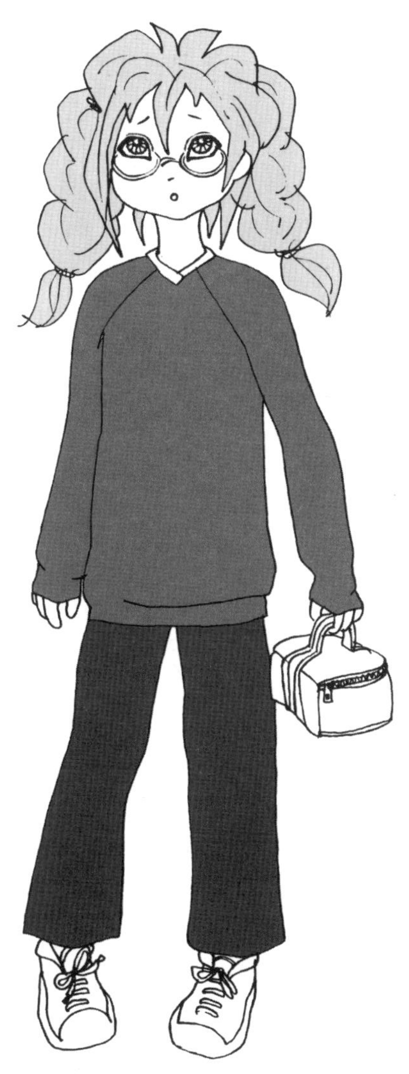

THE NEXT DAY ...
Hello, Mr. Townsend.
Hi. You must be Mr. Rivers.
Hi. Call me Tom.
Claire's inside. She's setting everything up for you.

Hello, Sky.
Come on in to the bakery for a coffee, Tom.
Better not. I've got two sick boys on my hands, so I have to head right back. Thanks, anyway.

You've got everything set up.
I found a bunch of little trees and farm animals from Dad's old train set. We can put the pond here with the well.
Maybe we should use a little dowsing rod so we put it in the right place.
A dowsing rod?
You know, a stick that water witches use to find water.

There's no such thing as witches.
No, but that's what they call people who find underground streams by using a stick.
That's impossible.
Honest. I'll show you. C'mon outside.

First we get a branch
that looks like a wishbone.
Like this!

Now what? I thought you said it only works for water witches.

I am a water witch!

Lots of people are water witches and don't even know it.
Here, you try it. It will twitch if there's water underground.
How does it work?

We need a new well because the water from the lake is polluted.
I thought only cities got polluted. How does a lake get polluted way out there?
My dad said that a big company has been dumping waste into our lake for years.
Why doesn't anybody stop them?

No one can prove it. And people keep getting sick.
Like those two boys from your lake who are always absent?
My brother, Jayden, and my cousin Jonathan.
How awful.
They're getting better. But it's like we're being poisoned.
Someone has to stop them.

Oh, look! The stick is moving!
Yes, it's twitching! There must be water underground.
Does this mean I can find water?
Yes, you're a real water witch!
I wonder if it's good for finding anything else. I lost a bird whistle out here this summer.

Dear Diary:

Guess what! We got an A+ for our diorama! It turned out fantastic. (No thanks to Jet.) Tabby and Erica were GREEN with envy.

To celebrate, Sky's dad has invited us to Lovesick Lake next Sunday for their Wild Earth Festival. It's a fundraiser to help pay for the community's new water well. Mom and Dad said we worked so hard on our project we deserve to go, and Jet's mom agreed. I can't wait! I'm going to take my whole science kit so I can make notes on new species for my scrapbook.

Claire

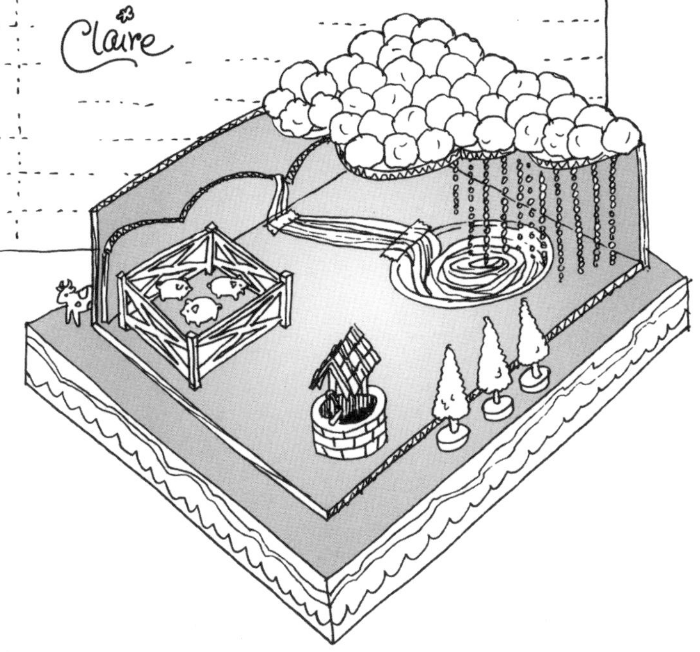

EARLY NEXT SUNDAY ...
We're here!
Wow, you all made it. Come and see what my mom's making!
I'm so glad you came.
Claire, this is my mom.

So you're the clever girl who made the rain project. Sky has been talking about it nonstop.
Nice to meet you, Mrs. Rivers.
And this is Jet.
Sky told us you're going to be a famous photographer.

Good idea. But be back in an hour for lunch or you'll be starving by suppertime.

Mom's making mooseburgers.

Sounds delicious ...

Sounds dangerous.

Oh, Lovesick Lake is beautiful.
Let's go fishing! Can we, Sky?
We used to fish all the time, but Dad won't let us anymore. The fish are bad.
Is it because of what you said about the water?

Yes. It used to be so blue and full of fish and ducks and loons.
It's kind of a smelly green.
I guess it is a bit icky.
Oh, I didn't mean that. Let me take some photos of you and your lake.

No, I don't want my picture taken.
C'mon. The flowers on your shirt will look good against the lake.
Wow, really? I brought my pink sweater, too.
Coming, Claire?

I'm here to enjoy nature, not watch a fashion show.

I'm going back to the community center.

Yessir, this is your top bird in firefighting. I can survey ten times the area I used to cover from the lookout.
And we hear you in the sky all the time now, Ranger Rhonda.
Hey, she's not that noisy!
Hi, hon. Having fun?
Where are the girls?
Oh. Jet's taking pictures. Again.

She's driving everyone nuts.
There's no harm in it.
It's not like she's taking pictures of nature. She wants to be a fashion photographer. How boring.
It's her way of making friends.
Shallow friends who just want to be models or something.
Oh, Claire, it's just a phase. She's having fun ...
C'mon inside, Grumpy. There's a drumming session you're gonna love. And lunch is almost ready.

INSIDE THE COMMUNITY CENTER ...
Where are the girls? It's not like Jet to miss lunch.
Sigh. I think Jet's mad at me.
I guess I haven't been very nice to her lately.
But she's driving me crazy with her photography.

I know. But that doesn't mean you're not best friends.
Really?
I'll bet Jet is not mad at you at all.
Okay. If you think so. C'mon, Bongo. Let's go find Jet.
We'll be right back.

YOO-HOO-OO-OO

VIEW

PING!

Oh, no!
They're in trouble.
But where did
they go?

Hmmm.
Maybe a water witch could find a clue ...
Oh, look, Bongo!

And there's another!
They're beads from Jet's ugly bag!
Arf!
Good boy!

I don't see any more beads.
Maybe she ran out of them.
I wish that camera bag were bigger.
I can't believe I said that.
Hey, where are you going?

MEANWHILE ...

It's not working.

Let me try. I think it's supposed to be a stick and a rock, not two sticks.

No. It's two sticks.
You take —

Someone's
coming ...

BONGO!
Come back!
CLAIRE!

I knew you'd find us.
I just knew it.
I saw your beads and followed the trail.
You were so smart to rip the beads off your bag to make a trail.
You were so smart to follow them!
We want to alert Ranger Rhonda. But I can't get a fire going.

Let me try.
Needs more gum wrappers!

You won't believe what happened to us.
Yes, I would. It's all in here!
My camera! You found my camera!

And I saw the pictures.
Of those awful people dumping in my lake?
And coming after you ...
Yeah, when they saw us ...
I screamed and ran into the bush.

That's when I dropped the camera. We ran and ran.
And they chased and chased us.
But we climbed up a tree and hid in the branches.
We sat way up and didn't make a sound.

Oh, my gosh.
They didn't see you?
They didn't look up. We could hear them talking.
They said they had to hurry back to dump another load and couldn't waste any more time on two dumb kids.

We wanted to go after them. But by then I had run out of beads, so we couldn't find our way back to the road.

But we found this clearing and decided to try to send a sign to Ranger Rhonda.

It must have been so scary.

But so fantastic because we discovered who is polluting Sky's lake.

I know! You were really brave to take these pictures. Just like a photojournalist.
See. You thought I was just taking silly pictures.
No, I didn't.
Yes, you did.
Did not.
Did.
I think I'll go get more firewood. Come with me, Bongo.

I'm sorry if I was a little crabby.
You were a lot crabby.
I thought you were more interested in Erica and Tabby.
Well, you were busy with Sky.
She's nice, but you'll always be my best friend.
Best Forever Friends?
Yup. Best Friends Forever.

This should keep the fire going. I brought some damp leaves to make smoke.
Fantastic!
Now I guess all we can do is wait
... and hope.

BUT SOON ...
Look! It's Ranger Rhonda's firefighter helicopter! Help me douse the fire.
Ranger Rhonda!
Ranger Rhonda!
Ruff Ruff!

Get in and buckle up!
Let's get you girls home. Your parents are worried sick.

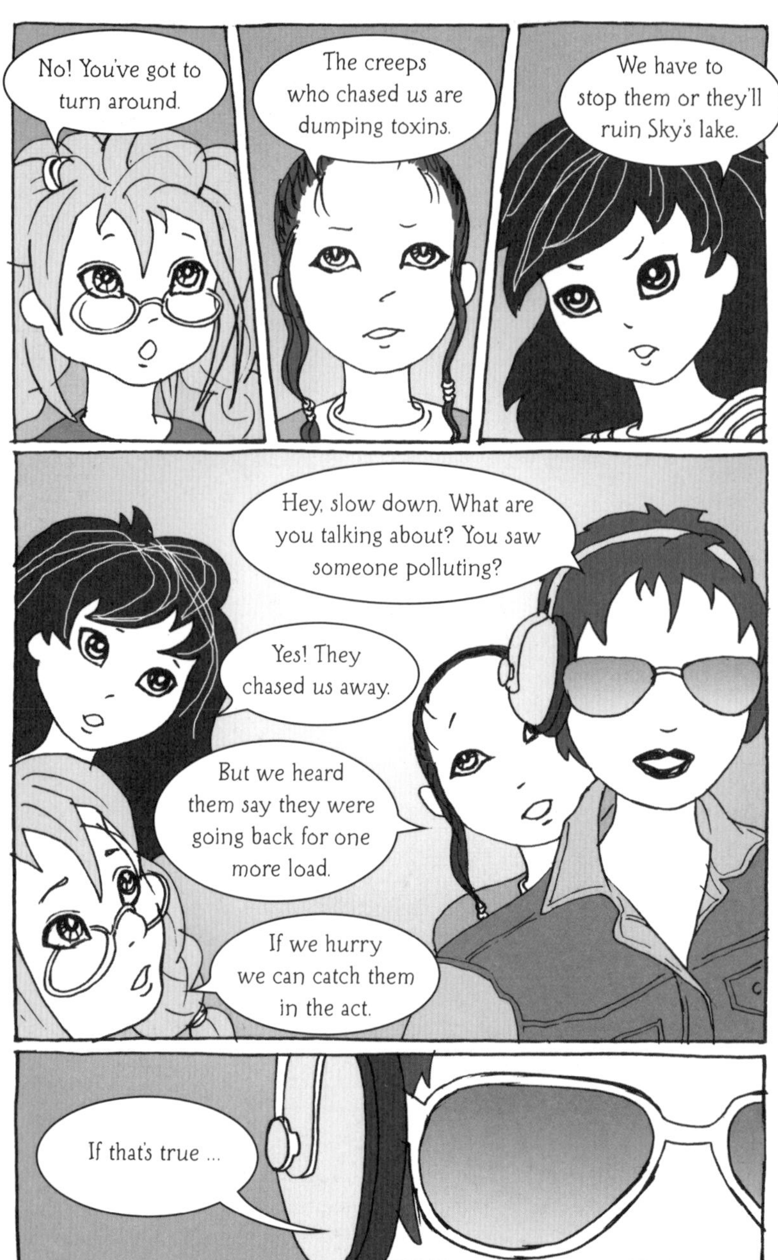
No! You've got to turn around.
The creeps who chased us are dumping toxins.
We have to stop them or they'll ruin Sky's lake.
Hey, slow down. What are you talking about? You saw someone polluting?
Yes! They chased us away.
But we heard them say they were going back for one more load.
If we hurry we can catch them in the act.
If that's true ...

From the Copter
To Officer Bob
SQUAWK
CLICK
BUZZ
Let's do it!
Sit tight, girls. We're going after them.
WOO HOO!
woof woof

MOMENTS LATER ...
MEGAPIG FEEDLOTS

Why not?
We can't go too much closer.
They can probably hear my copter. If I stay wide, they'll think I'm just on my regular rounds. We have to wait for Officer Bob.
They won't be here long.
I've already got pictures of them dumping. We just have to catch them loading waste from MegaPig.
You're right, Jet! Give me your camera. I've got an idea.

Go in as close as you can, Ranger Rhonda.
I can take zoomed-in photos to get the proof we need.

PERPS HEADING NORTH ON 50 IN A PURPLE PICK-UP.

ROGER, RHONDA.
ETA IN FIVE.

Claire!

Sky!

Dad!

Claire, again, I must remind you. Apprehending criminals is better left to the police.

Promise me that you will stay out of these dangerous situations.

And that goes double for you two.

And it's all because of your dumping.

It can't be that bad for the lake.

If you saw the diorama we made for Ms. Beene, you would know better.

What's a diorama?

You two will have plenty of time to look it up in the jailhouse library.

Along with your buddies from MegaPig FeedLots.

Dear Diary:

It's been so exciting. The people from the newspaper and TV have been calling us nonstop for interviews. I've promised to sew every single jewel back onto Jet's camera bag so she can wear it on TV.

Dad is taking us into the city tomorrow so we can go to court and hear the verdict. We are learning a lot about how the justice system works. Sky is thinking of becoming a lawyer, and now Jet wants to be a newspaper photographer. I think I'll stick with zoology. It's not as beastly.

Claire

Jet's Crafts for Future Famous Photographers

Taking photos is fun. But don't just let them sit in an album or on your computer. Make cool stuff like this and share it with your friends.

You probably have a lot of the materials you will need at home. Remember to get permission to use them.

Tiny Photo Tags

Hang these on your school bag or lunch box or anywhere you want mini pictures of your friends.

These little framed photos are made with metal rim key tags found anywhere keys are cut and at office supply stores. Look for ball chain at hardware stores.

YOU WILL NEED

two photos
a 25-cent coin
a pencil
scissors
a paint brush
white glue
water
a small container
a plastic spoon
a 3.175 cm (1 1/4 in.) round metal rim key tag
two 7 cm (2 3/4 in.) lengths of ball chain

1. Choose an area of the first photo you wish to put on your tag. Using the coin as a guide, trace a circle around that area and cut it out.

2. Position the photo on the key tag and trim if necessary to allow the key ring to move freely in the hole.

3. Prepare glue mixture by stirring four spoons of glue and one spoon of water together in a small bowl. Brush one side of the key tag with the glue mixture and immediately press the photo on top, centering it on the tag. Allow to dry for 5 minutes, then apply another coat of glue mixture over the photo and up to the metal rim.

4. Squeeze a thin line of white glue between the photo and the rim. Using a toothpick, position the ball chain into a ring around the photo. Allow to dry, then brush liberally with another coat of glue mixture. Allow to dry overnight.

5. Repeat on the reverse side.

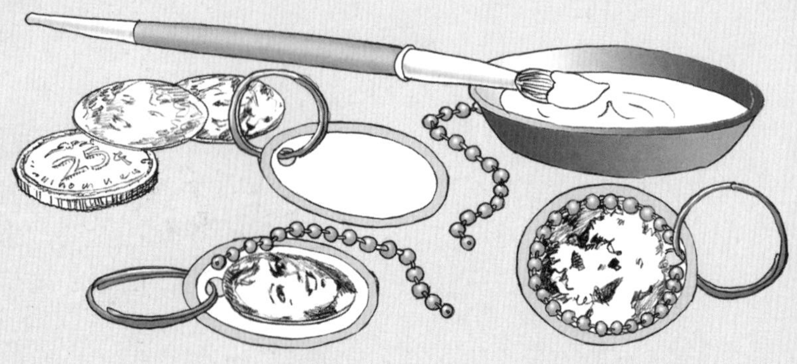

Claire's Jewel Case Frame

Recycle an old CD case to make a bedazzled frame for your favorite photo.

YOU WILL NEED

a discarded CD case with CD
white glue
a small container
assorted beads, buttons and jewels
tweezers

1. Remove CD and album cover from the case and set aside.

2. Pour a small amount of white glue into the container. One at a time, dip beads and jewels into the glue and position them around the border of the case, using the tweezers if necessary. Leave the center area undecorated so your photo will show through. Set aside to dry.

3. In the meantime, select a photo or a picture from a magazine. Using the album cover as a guide, trace a square on the image, then cut it out.

4. Place the trimmed picture in the case and snap closed.

Accordion Photo Album

You can display LOTS of pictures in Claire's Jewel Case Frame by making this accordion photo album.

YOU WILL NEED

Claire's Jewel Case Frame
the discarded CD
a pencil
2 sheets colored construction paper
scissors
5 photos with a 13 cm x 13 cm (5 in. x 5 in.) image area
a glue stick
1 60-cm (23-in.) length of ribbon

1. Using the CD as a guide, trace four circles on the colored paper, and cut them out. Do the same with the photos, centering the circles on the areas that you like the most.

2. Line up the CD and the colored paper circles so they are side by side without overlapping.

3. Run the glue stick along the length of one side of the ribbon.

4. Place the ribbon, glue side down, on the CD and paper circles, connecting them along their middles. Trim off any excess ribbon.

5. Apply glue to the ribbon, the CD and the colored paper circles. Place your photo circles on top of the CD and the paper circles, sandwiching the ribbon. Set aside to dry.

6. When the glue has dried, you can write a fun description on the colored paper backing of each photo. Place the CD back into the case, photo side up, and press to snap into place. Accordion-fold the photos on top of each other and snap the case closed.